Educating Children on Death

Dr. Deborah Hollimon
Artwork: Dr. Deborah Hollimon

ISBN 978-1-0980-5090-0 (paperback)
ISBN 978-1-0980-5091-7 (hardcover)
ISBN 978-1-0980-5093-1 (digital)

Christian Faith Publishing, Inc.
832 Park Avenue
Meadville, PA 16335
www.christianfaithpublishing.com

Artwork: Dr. Deborah Hollimon

Printed in the United States of America

A ngel and Grandpa would take many walks together. Angel enjoyed these walks with his grandpa. It gave Angel time to know his grandpa better. Angel loved his grandpa.

Grandpa and Angel loved playing hide-and-seek. They would both look forward to playing this game.

"Angel, count again to ten. It takes me longer to walk due to my stiff legs."

"Okay, Grandpa."

So Angel counted, "One, two, three…" up to ten again.
Angel was so excited when Grandpa said, "I am ready.
Come and catch me."

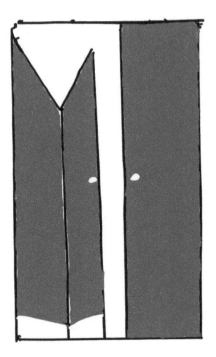

Angel searched the closet but could not find Grandpa.
He looked in the kitchen, but there was no Grandpa.
"Grandpa, where are you?"

"I am here, Angel!"

Grandpa and Angel would play video games together. Angel felt all grown-up, showing his Grandpa how to play the games.

Angel also enjoyed going to the library with Grandpa. There they would read books together. He also enjoyed getting a library card. Angel felt all grown-up!

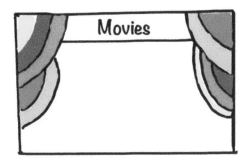

Angel and Grandpa enjoyed going to the movies together. They liked watching action and comedy movies the most.

Angel and Grandpa would also go to church. They would pray together and thanked God for all their blessings. Grandpa taught Angel that he could go to God and talk to him about anything.

School Cafeteria

Angel and Grandpa would enjoy going to the school cafeteria. Here grandpa would come and eat with Angel. He was able to tell Grandpa what he did at school that day. Angel also introduced his school friends to Grandpa.

Angel enjoyed going to the park with Grandpa. At the park they played ball together. They both had lots of fun.

Then one day Angel called out for Grandpa but did not see him. He then ran to his mommy and asked her what happened to his Grandpa.

She explained that Grandpa was having problems with his heart and had to be taken quickly to the hospital. Angel's mother promised him that she would take him to see his grandpa.

That did not happen. A call came from the hospital staff saying that Grandpa had passed on. Angel did not know what this was all about. He asked his mother what did this mean.

His mother told him that Grandpa was no longer physically here with him. She said, "Angel, there are two parts of us when we are born, a spiritual part, which we cannot see, and a physical part that we can see. Grandpa had removed the physical part and now is back in heaven to do God's work with him."

"Angel, do you understand?" his mommy asked.
"Yes, Mommy, Grandpa finished his work here on earth for God and is helping God back in heaven."

"So when can I see him again, Mommy?"

"When you finish your work on earth and God calls you back home."

Angel appeared very sad and started to cry.

Mommy told Angel, "It is okay to feel sad and cry." She hugged and kissed Angel on his forehead. Mommy also said to Angel, "Grandpa is still here in spirit. One of the ways you can connect to Grandpa is by writing to him. Other ways to connect with Grandpa are to look out for signs. Things that both of you shared together."

Mommy then gave a journal for Angel to write in. Mommy then told Angel. "I love you very much, my son."

Angel replied, "Thank you, Mommy."

"I miss you, Grandpa!

I am writing to you!

Hope you are okay?"

"I am fine. I am helping God in heaven!
I love you!
Keep writing and talking to me.
I am with you always!"

"Remember you can write to Grandpa anytime, Angel.
Here is a notebook you can write in."
"Thank you, Mommy."

Mommy told Angel to look out for the signs from heaven. "Angel, you both liked butterflies. This is one of the signs telling you that Grandpa is okay."

"Or you may hear a favorite tune that you both liked to listen to. You know, Angel, your favorite tune?"

"Yes, Mommy. I will look out for it."

"Mommy, can we play hide-and-seek like Grandpa used to?"

"Yes, Angel, my darling," Mommy said. "Let's start now. One, two, three…"

Angel then went to hide.

We are all back together again in heaven!

The End

Do read our book entitled, *Educating Children on Divorce.*

Please accept this rose from the author.

About the Author

Greetings!

I am a family nurse practitioner with a doctor's degree in nursing. My purpose for writing my series of books for children is to give them a platform to connect with various life issues, such as death. I find that a lot of children, parents, and caretakers do not know how to begin a conversation about such issues. By reading this book, the child will feel comfortable in talking about death with his parents or caregivers.

Enjoy reading with your child the book entitled *Educating Children on Death*. Also look out for the book entitled *Educating Children on Divorce*.

Thank you.

Printed in the USA
CPSIA information can be obtained
at www.ICGtesting.com
LVHW060926190124
769161LV00067B/88

9 781098 050917